Naught s

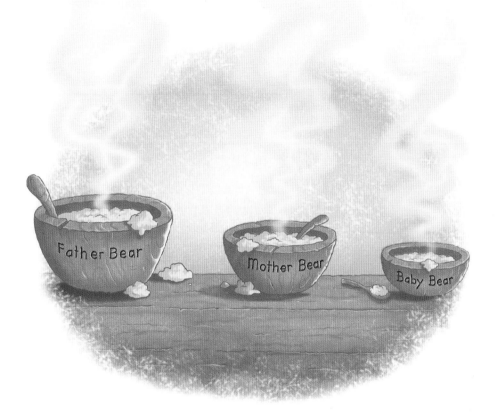

retold by Pam Holden
illustrated by Richard Hoit

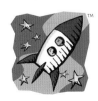

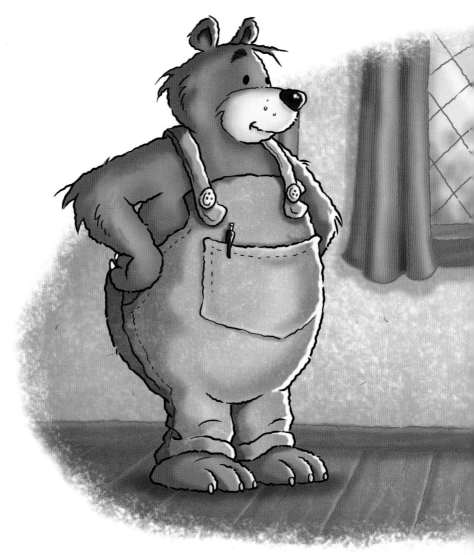

B is for bears.

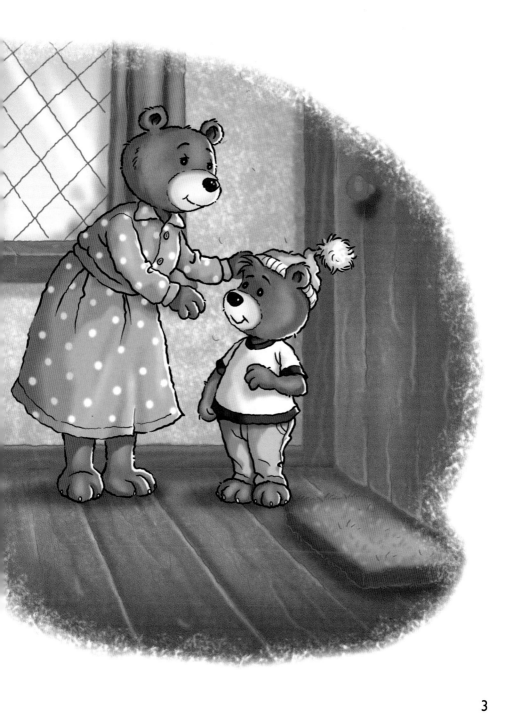

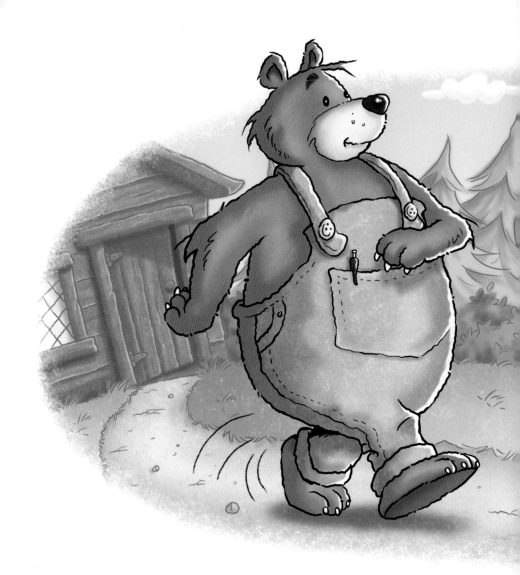

W is for walk.

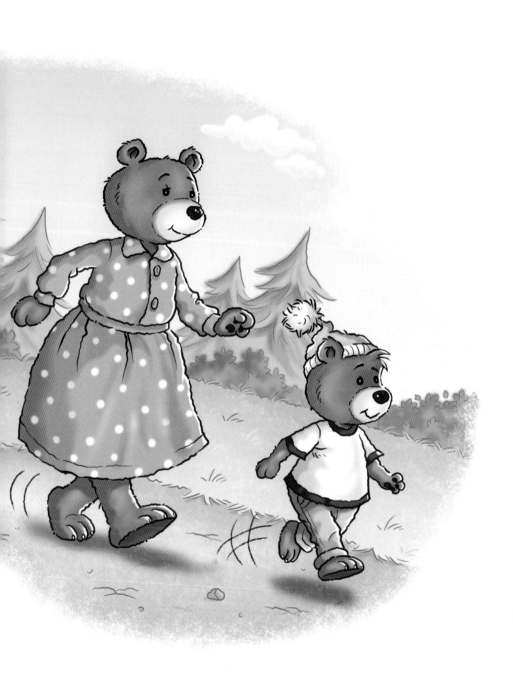

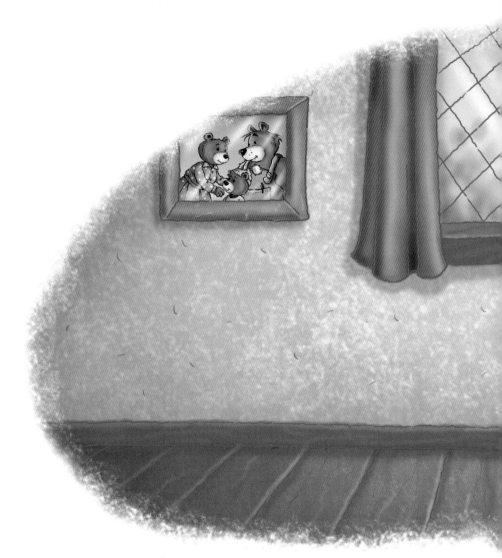

D is for door.

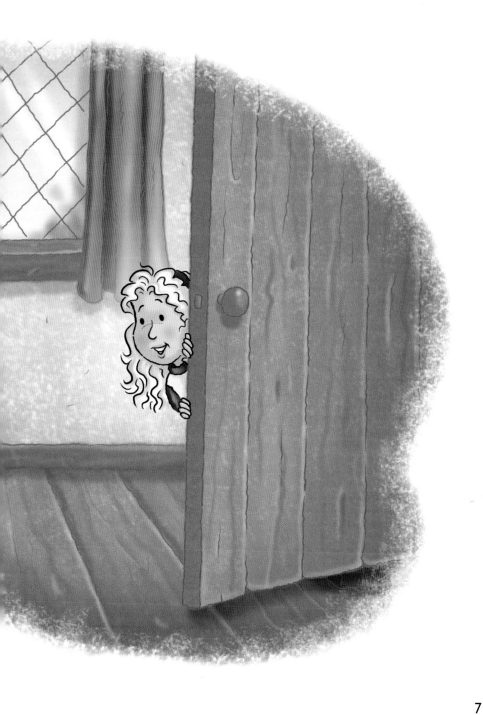

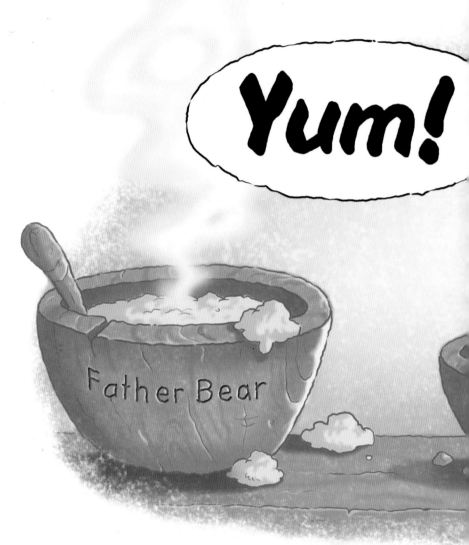

P is for porridge.

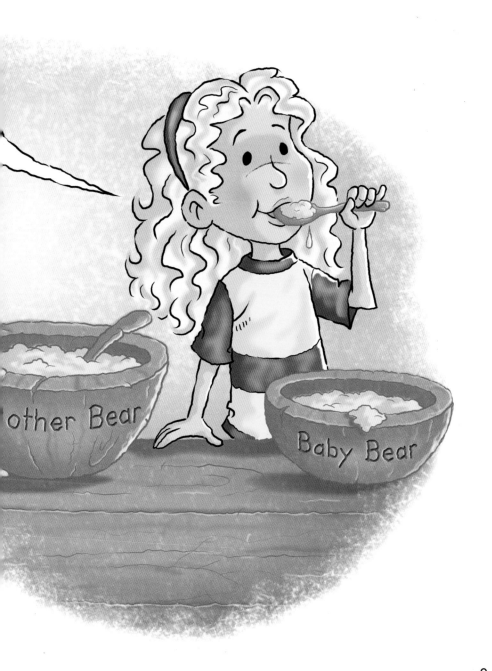

other Bear

Baby Bear

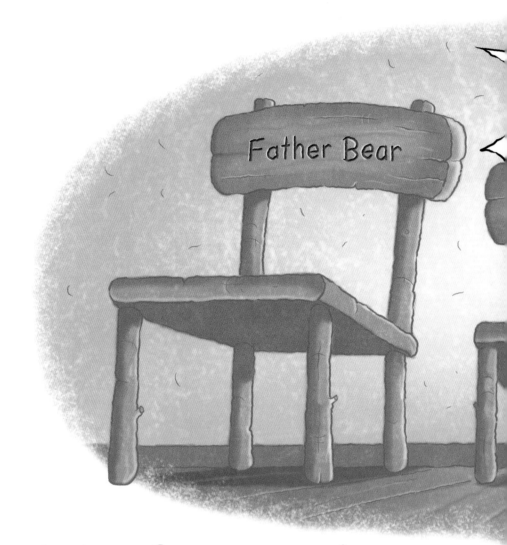

C is for crash.

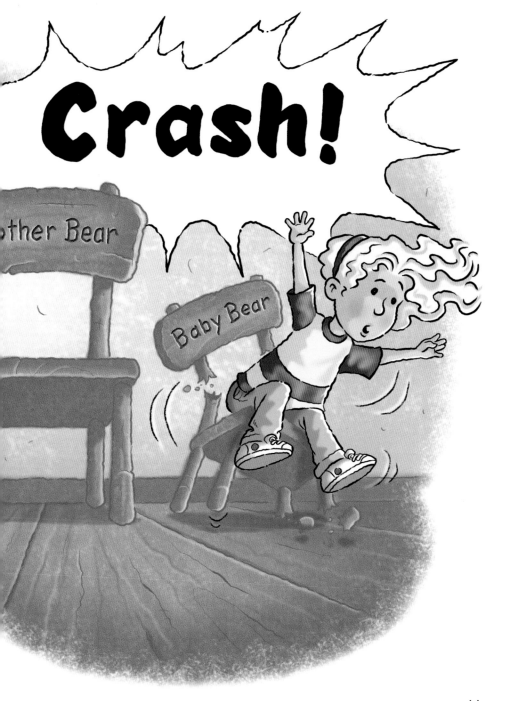

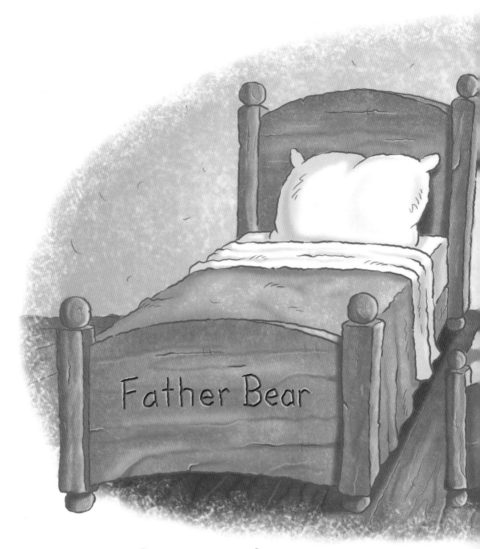

S is for sleep.

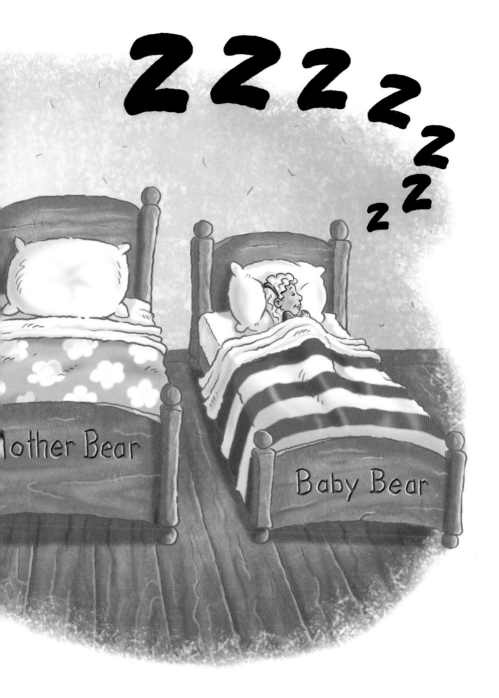

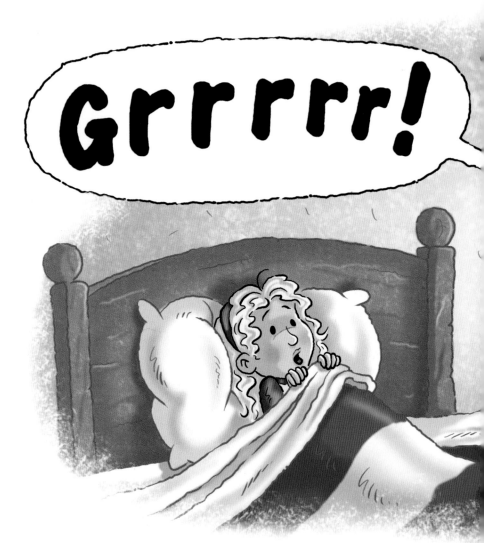

G is for growl.

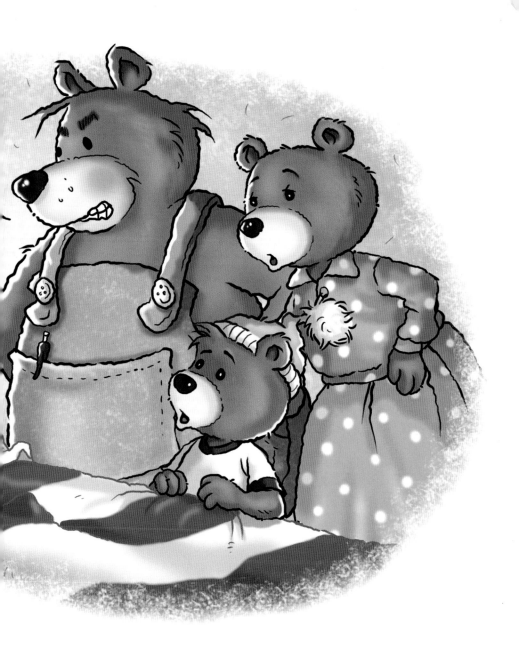

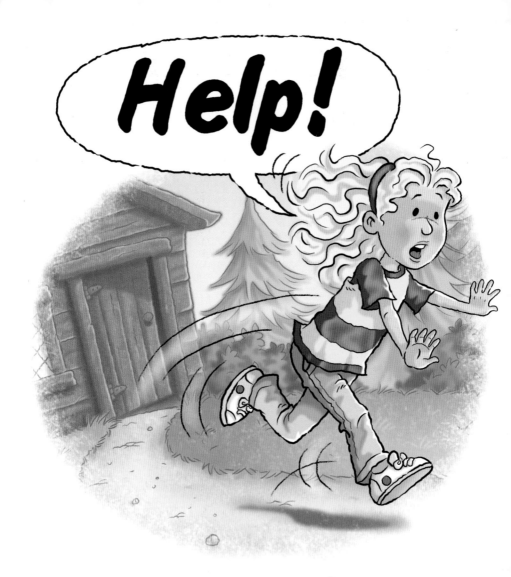

R is for run!